EXORCISTS OF THE CRIMSON ORDER

A FANTASY STORY

JONATHAN EVAN HUDSON

EXORCISTS OF THE CRIMSON ORDER

CHAPTER I

ROO DE BLADES

Trouble often came in threes and the giant wall of bright white stone all around the town of Twin Pearl, the first real trouble Roo de Blades had to face today.

The wall towered at least a hundred feet high. Maybe more. High enough that climbing over it during the day ... not the best idea, and climbing it tonight—no. It was noon already. Night was too far away. Far too many hours away.

Roo didn't have the time to wait. Not now. Not yet.

Not until he learned more about the coming attack—and how to stop it.

He was an Exorcist of the Crimson Order, after all—one of humanity's last hopes against the monsters waging war against them. From enraged witches to vicious vampires. From wicked werewolves to murderous mummies.

Even dastardly dragons.

Especially dastardly dragons. Especially those who could shift into a human form.

So Roo better be prepared to fight them—one and all.

But the wall itself was sheered so too sleek. Shiny sleek under the bright noon sun. Blindingly sleek. As if the stone was actually some kind of metal. Not a cloud in the sky either. Just like there was not a single handhold along that whole entire round wall.

Not one. Obvious or not.

Not at all.

So too sleek for a night climb. Least for now.

Least Crooster flew over it easily enough. Acting like some ordinary crow of course—but still, that was near dawn. Now it was near noon. And he hadn't returned.

Not yet.

But no worries. Much.

Years together with Crooster playing his familiar, a creature bonded through a special magical contract to be loyally devoted to and protective of its master, taught Roo that that shapeshifting crow could escape most trouble easily.

And the moat for this town. The town of Twin Pearl.

Like too many towns throughout the land of Greenwell, the moat hugged the white stone. A moat a loooong dozen paces wide. A moat clogged with thickets of sinister dark-green seaweed so thick those feathery tendrils would drown the finest of swimmers and quickly too.

No mermaids need apply either. The seaweed would definitely drown them too.

And then, for another several dozen paces beyond the

moat, hard packed dirt as dark and green as the moat itself. Before rolling hills of short stiff ankle-high grass swept over for miles and miles around.

Until a carpet of a pine forest sprouted up in the far, far, faaaar distance.

So far away those crazy tall pines actually looked like meager little finger-long spears clustered together into a spikey carpet.

And these hills rolled down and over and down some more.

The town was on a tall hill after all. More than tall enough to get lesser men huffing and puffing seriously way too much if they foolishly took the direct route up, and not the road weaving around and around and around the hill, up to the wall.

And Roo, he was no fool—despite the stray ... comment from Crooster.

Roo was just in a hurry. Yes. A very great and big hurry.

No time to enjoy the scenery, as his dad would lightheartedly say.

Or stop and smell the weeds, as his mom would jokingly say.

Worse Roo better not reveal his Exorcist identity right away. Until Crooster returned there was no telling who or what really controlled the town—humans or something else, or even humans serving something else, or ...

Roo took another deep patient breath.

That crunchy solid grass, it all was cut fresh and often, judging by the strong smell if it. Obviously to keep anyone, or anything from using it to hide as they approached the walls.

Not by magic—or else just looking at it would at least tingle his hackles, if not his eyes.

So nothing hid that loooong line to reach the drawbridge. As in several loops around the wall, and the hill itself, long.

A line Roo was next in line for, *finally*—after arriving long before the crack of dawn

But such long lines into walled towns during troubled times wasn't exactly unusual. Back as a little kid, back when he traveled with his mom and dad, back when they were both alive and worked as bards, Roo spend way too much time on such lines.

And learned early on that getting there early was critical to getting into town at all.

And the drawbridge here at Twin Pearl was still actually lowered across the moat.

Only a couple few feet above the moat the drawbridge itself was a slab of thick oak planks warped dark gray and so creaky old and wobbly even the weak breeze here made it squeak like a horde of dying mice.

But the only way to get through that arched gateway into Twin Pearl proper.

Thankfully an empty drawbridge, of course, no line on it, since no crossing the drawbridge without approval first ... so no skipping that much.

Yet.

Roo went with a heavy-cotton pale-blue body-covering

shawl with a hood over his head, hiding his sky-blue hair and its dark-blue streaks near his scalp—his natural weird hair color due to some elven blood in him, but not enough to count as a proper elf, or even a real half elf.

Least not by actual elves.

No pointy ear thing like his quarter-elf dad. No fruity stink like his half-elf mom.

Nothing like that.

So Roo dyed his hair black. Pitch black. Matching Crooster.

Just in case.

Since this shawl also hid his actual Exorcist uniform as well. Hid that fancy crimson vest over a crisp white shirt and crimson-red slacks. Long droopy sleeves hid most of his fingerless gloves and the emblem on the back of those gloves.

White on what looked like worn-down crimson suave.

Three concentric circles. A cross over the inner two circles.

The emblem of an Exorcist of any order.

Only his pitch-black boots of soft leather were still visible. The magic woven into his entire uniform gave his whole body far more durability, more resistance to magic and to the elements than a regular human, or most suits of armor.

And more importantly it ensured only monsters would really notice, would really remember him.

(As long as he wasn't too tired. It drained his stamina slowly but steadily while doing so.)

Even while wearing this regular nothing-special shawl.

Even with the long droopy sleeves over his fingerless crimson gloves of what looked like worn-down crimson suave—his infinity gloves might give him away.

But these gloves were also part of his uniform, and magical. Powerfully magical. They could store a near infinite amount of things. Let him draw them nearly instantly—or slow and steadily.

And the need to draw any of his weapons instantly was more critical.

Even now.

Especially now.

Especially without his partner around yet.

As a sword shifter, she could shift herself, part or in whole, into a wickedly wonderful saber that could slice and dice through and even deflect most kinds of magic. He struggled to wield her properly since you know, most elves thought themselves above any mere human.

Especially a human with only a little elven blood in them.

She hesitated to even let him touch her.

At all.

So yeah. Troublesome to say the least.

Still this was all needed to hide the fact he was an Exorcist. Least for now. Assess the situation without drawing the wrong kind of attention. Monsters weren't the only troublemakers, sometimes, and not all monsters were troublemakers either.

Some were even Exorcists too.

So Roo would pose as a starving artist of the bard kind—with or without Crooster in toe.

Yeah. So try getting approval first. If that fails ... let's burn that can of worms later. If it came to that.

A big if.

CHAPTER 2
ROO DE BLADES

Too big an if.

Almost as big as the chest on this elf girl guard before, and beside the drawbridge, and wowzer, did this utterly gorgeous elf girl guard have a nice chest on her. Inhumanly humanly beautiful she was.

A peach pie for the eyes and loins.

Especially in that bright-green minidress of sleeveless beauty, of stretchy-leather-like whatever stretched and hugging her like Roo kinda sortof wanted to. It was so amazingly ultrasnug, so form-fitting, so stretchy supple that it left no amazingly hourglassy curve of hers to the imagination.

So damn. did that sight make the hot day even hotter.

Steamingly hot

Hot enough that a dive together into that wide moat would have been nice—except for all that thick dense seaweed clogging it dangerously deadly.

Noon sun in the cloudless sky nonwithstanding. Nonwithstanding at all.

Never mind her low-heeled shin boots as they tapped the hard-packed dark-green dirt. Tapping as if keeping the beat to a song she was singing all and only to herself.

Not annoyed-with-him tapping.

Not yet.

Boots with an extra-wide lighter-dark-green sleeve stylishly hanging over most of the inner dark-green sleeve. So yeah, stylish in a pretty pricey kinda way. Too pricy for the average town guard of any sort.

And as a guard she had to be armed, of course.

How else could she stop just anyone from dashing across this flimsy drawbridge?

Beside the obvious threat of that creaky wobbly slab of planks falling apart if stepped on even slightly too hard. Never mind it was only a few couple feet above the moat. The moat itself was deadly enough.

But the arched gateway was wide open. No other obvious other guard in sight.

Yet.

Only several paces of gateway tunnel through the stone wall—a tunnel arched nearly a dozen paces high at its highest point—before a gap of several paces for a few-pace-wide street of white stone. And then another wall of solid white stone.

No other guard. As weird as that was.

Or maybe not.

Since strapped to her sexy slim waist was a nice pair of

sleek sabers. Each with an inch-wide blade curved slightly upward. Each sheathed entirely in thick lime-green leather.

A twin blade wielder? As a guard? Weird ...

Wielding twin blades properly took some serious training —whether magical blades or not. Roo could manage it. Barely. After lots and lots of training from mom, dad, and ... others. Even with blades alive and willing to help him. It took enough skill that it would take far more pay than a typical town guard could make for guarding a drawbridge so —woh.

The nice warm breeze in his face. It washed her scent into his face too.

Not just the river-watery smell of wet fresh seaweed.

But wow, like a whole bowl of nice fresh ripe black cherries. Perfect on this steamingly hot day.

But like any elf girl, she smelled of some kind of fruit, so nothing special there.

Ripe fruit usually. No idea why, yet. but so what?

Her pair of pigtails, woh, were like wonderous fountains of bright ruby-red hair off the left and right top sides of her head. So no hiding at all how those ears were so amazingly elven, that they were shaped kinda sortof like few-inch daggers jutting from the sides of her head.

That lovely heart of a beautiful baby face smiled cheerfully at him that very moment.

A smile from her lovely ruby-red lips actually reached up to those glowingly-bright sky-blue eyes of hers. Nice and beautifully big eyes streaked with sparkling hints of mesmerizing lime green.

Those glowingly bright eyes—not unheard of, more like not unseen from monsters hiding as elves, or even as humans.

"And you are ..." she said.

Her voice was like honey made into lyrical sound.

But so what? That was a very common elf girlish kind of thing. Even his elf girl partner who shall remain as nameless as she was late had it too—whether in elven form or in sword form.

Still the friendliness in this elf girl's voice was ... weird.

Heart-racingly wonderfully ... weird.

Elves looked down on human anything. Treating humans as ugly bugs more or less.

Like she had treated the elderly couple in front of Roo.

And the pudgy merchant with a small barrel of cart ahead of the elderly couple.

Especially elf girls to human guys—or any guy with enough non-elf blood in them.

That's why his partner, a certain elf girl who shall remain as nameless as she was late, refused to travel alone with him, him being too unworthy of her isolated presence or some horse-shit like that.

Despite her being the sword Headquarters assigned him to wield.

Least for the next few many missions.

Crooster nonwithstanding. Since crows, apparently, even shapeshifting magical crows didn't count. Least to that elf girl.

Never mind that Crooster had secrets of his very own—including a human form.

More like a powerful wizard form.

Not that he was a wizard.

Nope.

Not at all.

Okay, okay. Starving bard time.

And what starving bard didn't load on the charm to any pretty lass he could lay his charm on? And this lass, wow did he want to load the charm onto her, and then some.

Prove that other elf girl wrong wrong wrong.

Never mind the groans and moans from the line behind him. A line weaving around and around and around the wall, and the hill, and maybe beyond the hill by now.

"You are," Roo said, "far too lovely for words alone."

So Roo granted this pigtailed cutie a deep nice bow of courtesy.

"I'm Rowan la Mayhem, at your service. Call me Roo. My friends—and lovers—do so."

Of course that wasn't his real name. His real name was Romeo de Blades. Technically a lost prince of sorts from so somewhere far away none of it really mattered, since mom ... well ... that whole royal thing with her ... she never went too far into it, so, of course, not important.

Not then. Not now.

Only his usual nickname was actually Roo.

But the pigtailed cutie clearly giggled enough to jiggle that big chest of hers nice and jiggly—completely unaware of his lie. So no vampire blood in her. Or witch blood either.

Either could detect intentional lies easily enough.

"And I'm Tinselletta Sparkles," she said. "Call me Tinsel. So Roo, what's your business here at Twin Pearl?"

Second weird thing ... Twin Pearl was very much a human town. No elves interested. Not at all. Even his nameless partner. Especially his elf girl partner.

Usually.

And yet here one was. An actual elf girl on guard duty for a human town.

If she really was an elf girl.

Big if.

An if as big as her chest, actually.

"Cute name there, Tinsel," Roo said. "A name as cute as you are."

More giggles and wow, that chest-jiggling giggle of hers, it was as cheerfully sweet as any honeyed mead—and just as intoxicating.

"Roo's an adorable name too," Tinsel said. "So what's your business here, Roo? Besides seducing pretty lasses like me, he-he."

Her cheeks even flushed red a touch. His natural charm. Working wonders already.

Unlike what that elf girl partner who shall remained nameless believed.

Or, even more close by, the groaning whoever right behind Roo.

"I'm a starving artist," Roo said, "of the bard kind. My art, painting stories in song—"

"Can't pay the toll then," Tinsel said.

Not a question either.

"Well, true," Roo said, "but—"

"No butts," Tinsel said, "except yours looking elsewhere to beg. Soooorrriiiiieeeee💔 But rules **are** rules, and—"

"My art is *not* begging!" Roo said. "It is—"

"For wooing girls like me," Tinsel said, "into pay your bills."

Again, not a question, but than again, no anger in her voice either? Uh huh ...

The moans and groans of the crowd waiting behind him—critics best ignored.

"Boyfriend trouble is it?" Roo said. "Drop the dud and—"

"Pick up the bum?" Tinsel said.

Her palms now rested on the pommels of her sabers. Um. Okay ...

Tinsel sighed. "That's so stupidly crazy that ..."

But rather than argue Roo gave her his most charming playful smile and nod.

"Have a sweet tooth," Roo said, "for fun and song? For wandering under the fair blue sky?"

Tinsel tsked again, but so giggly and yet so skeptically that .... a little push and maybe—

"Enough is enough 🤍 🤍 🤍"

From a girl right behind Roo? Her voice—despite the impatience in it—like fresh honey poured on crisp slices of the ripest sweetest apples. And as lyrical as any elf girl ... if not more.

But the moment he turned and faced her—oh no,

The second serious trouble of the day. Right there. Right then.

CHAPTER 3
ROO DE BLADES

The erotic shock.

From the most erotic of gorgeous girls now before him. Yeah. Erotic.

Not just stunningly gorgeous like Tinsel there, behind him now, beside the wobbly creaky drawbridge of flimsy but thick planks, but wow, amazingly and stunningly erotic in her gorgeousness.

Ultra gorgeous.

Just the very sight of her. Like cool fresh lemonade on a steaming hot summer day.

And right now, wow, could Roo use a nice cold drink of lemonade. Not just to drink. But to dump over himself. Wow. Talk about a sight to overheat a guy dead still. Hourglass body to heaven, too heavenly, so heavenly it was all too easy never to return.

Thee perfect peach pie for the eye and loins.

The cloudless blue sky behind her. Radiant. So radiant it gave her a nice little blindingly bright aura too.

For a moment.

A quick blindingly perfect moment.

Wedges of hot-pink hair stylishly framed not just her heavenly heart of a beautiful baby face, but flowed straight down her sides and ended curled gracefully around a ginormous chest, a chest so colossal and yet sexy cute that ... wow.

Heavenly endowed she was ... was what his dad would have jokingly said.

Portrait perfect right there with that clear blue sky cloudless behind her.

Especially how that colossal chest of hers was strapped snuggly tight and amazingly exposed in that couple-inch wide hot-pink belt of amazingly shiny leather.

Its buckle. A hollow heart fashioned from a thick golden frame. Center of her chest too.

Not just the noon sun. Blazing down. Scorching him hot right here and now.

Wow.

Since that mesmerizing midriff of hers ... sexy slim and ... and amazingly woh. Wow. Nothing other than ... than ... a belt for a top?

Really?

Gulp.

Too.

Right.

Moans and groans nonwithstanding. From the whoevers behind her, far to the side, vary far to the side, out of sight far, so clearly giving her more than the usual space between people on a loooong line, a line so long it still wound around and around and around this very tall hill and walled town.

Because wow. Sure.

Sure. for. her neck. Her slim lovely neck ... an inch-wide collar of hot-pink leather with a similar hollow heart of a golden frame for a buckle.

Sure for her hands ... fingerless gloves of hot-pink leather —a palm-sized hollow heart of gold embedded on the very top of the hand of each glove. Her fingernails even shined hot pink with a ruby-red heart centered on each nail.

Slim pretty hands then fisting her hips. Hips now cocked sexy sideways.

Since sure her heart-stopping hips, her fantastically fit thighs, that low-hanging skirt ... so supershort and so super-snug, like ruby-red panties with a hot-pink skirt so stunningly ultrashort, and yet ...

Wait.

A few gooey bubbles popping out and around the moat nonwithstanding. From several paces away, nonwithstanding. The gooey pop sounds banging sharply against that towering high wall of white stone, nonwithstanding.

Around that ultrashort skirt of hers ... from the bottom to midway up it ... decorated with what looked like waves of shiny golden flames?

What the ... stylish but ... what the ... the shine, the sparkle.

Real gold?

Really?

And more gold. That hollow heart of a golden frame. It served as a buckle a couple inches too nicely big was ... well ...

Even more revealing.

Wow.

Undies-in-public kind of outfit practically, but in a stylish and very pricey way.

Just like those hot-pink shin boots grinding against the dark-green dirt below her. Ruby-red hearts laced with thin but sturdy golden chains chingled down the front insides of the sleeves, and on the bottom, thick dark-pink soles, but not high heels, but practical low heels.

Her deep hefty huff at Roo—that warm breath of hers, like she was chewing some kind of strawberry and vanilla candy—despite the fresh smell of her breath.

"Heeeey♥" she said. "Up here♥"

CHAPTER 4
JULIET HEARTEQUIN

J uliet Heartequin **could** *not* ***believe*** the nerve of the weird bard boy in front of her.

The way he ogled, he leered he down and over—how obvious, how long ... longer than this ridiculous line winding around and around and around this crazy tall hill. If not for her time magic and her ability to speed up time as much as she could slow it down for everyone, or anyone, (including herself, especially herself) in just a little area, or a huge area ...

Even halt time ...

Wow.

Upset would be an understatement.

If only her friends were here. If only ...

Felicia would so go wow over the towering high wall of white stone. Stone as pure amazing white as Felicia and that shapeshifting kitty cat's actual short fur coat in her true form.

Bubbles would so go ick at that wide moat so choked full of feathery seaweed.

At those stray bubbles that kept glopping up. Kept popping as loud, as icky as grandpop's smacking his overly wet lips.

Bubbles would so shift to her mermaid form on land, right then and there, leaving herself a superlovely golden-pigtailed elf girl on top, and shifting her hips and legs into a gorgeous hot-pink fish tail.

All to use her own magic at its most powerful.

Her ability to manipulate water in tons and tons of ways, simple or complex, to clean that odious moat up and make it sweet and swimmable again.

(If it was ever swimmable. Big if. But ... sigh.)

That weird note Bubbles suddenly and mysterious left for Juliet next to her bed ... not to tell anyone, saying to meet them in Twin Pearl of all places, after Bubbles and Felicia had vanished for several weeks, no sign or hint of where, no matter who looked for them ...

A note Juliet then couldn't even find. She read it, dropped it in shock and ... it vanished.

Completely.

How ... Felicia, Bubbles, neither had that kind of magic but ... sigh.

But Felicia would just **love** how creaky spooky that drawbridge was, especially how it was only a few feet above that icky moat and its planks seemed ready to fall apart any moment now.

As much as Felicia would love that drawbridge, Bubbles

would just **hate** it. Scared of ghosts or something silly like that—as silly as so many of her other friends, her witch friends getting more and more upset at humans for "reasons"—silly enough that Felicia would tease Bubble for it on and on and on just like Juliet did to her friends that whined about human this or that and "human menace" and other stupid stuff ...

Sigh.

As if ghosts were somehow different than any other monster out there ...

As if Juliet, Felicia, and even Bubbles weren't monsters themselves ...

As if witches weren't once human themselves ...

Even Juliet ... only a couple few year ago ... so some weird bard boy—no worries.

But if he wanted a fight like all her other friends said humans wanted, better be ready, especially if he's secretly one those monster hunting Exorcists that, supposedly, disappeared so many of her other friends that ...

Gulp.

This bard boy. As strangely cute as he was, and wow was he a smooth talker, the overly charming kind, the exact kind a girl had to be careful around.

Even if that ogling leer of his, ugh, he was as fresh as the cut grass around them, but probably just as harmless, but those gloves of his ... infinity gloves?

No need to question her instinct there. Not since she awakened as a witch.

A weird bard boy with infinity gloves ... weird.

He could afford infinity gloves but not a toll?

Really weird.

Unless .... he wasn't really a bard but a ... gulp, Exorcists, an exorcists out to trap and vanish witches like Juliet herself, so like grandpops said, don't start a fight, but be ready to end one, quickly, and conclusively.

Or else end up missing. Missing like so many of her friends lately.

CHAPTER 5

ROO DE BLADES

Oh yeah!

A quick look-over was fine with most girls but woh, Roo, his long tour of her wet-dream-fantasy-come-amazingly-true kind of heaven-endowed body in that erotic undies-in-public outfit, a big no no kinda ogle, more like outright leering, and woh, did Roo gulp before he could stop himself and looked back up and oh no.

On top of her head—that chilled tingle through his eyes and down his spine the moment he spotted it too, so definitely a witch hat of some sort. His hackles. Already too fried from sexy overheating of that ultra gorgeous wow that ...

Yup. A strangely unusual and yet very stylish hat ... a beret.

Yeah.

A stylishly snazzy unique kind of beret.

An extra-big, extra-floppy beret. Of extra-silky-fine and

smooth-looking wool. Amazingly shiny golden wool was woven like flames along the bottom up to bright hot-pink for the rest.

And embedded in the beret's front and center—a couple-inch-big heart-shaped ruby. Its many facets sparkled more and more with each and every movement of her head.

And clearly not just from the noon sun blazing straight down on them.

That ruby. A powerful magical gem, no doubt. Storing loads and loads of magic in it, since that eye-and-spine tingle, even his hackles cackled even more than before, and silently, but actually kinda painfully at the sight of that ruby.

No wonder no one was close behind her, or even near her sides, despite the lengthy line and all the impatient people lingering on it. Word of enraged witches engaging in wicked acts of retaliation for wrongs done since forever ...

Too common lately.

How many witches then enslaved other monsters as familiars to help do their dirty work?

Far too many lately.

And why a skilled elven guard might actually be paid enough to guard the gateway to a rich enough town. Twin Pearl wasn't exactly poor either. Plenty of merchants stopped by. Plenty of the trade routes passed through, or near the town.

An elf might not be willing to work with anyone else but an equally skilled elf.

So,. of course, only one guard here on duty.

Just in case an enraged witch did show up.

Like now—a potentially enraged witch out for trouble.

And that outfit, definitely a witch outfit. Not anywhere near the more modest dress, and definitely not the wide-brim and pointy crown kind of hat. Not at all.

Strange but so what? It was snazzy sexy too.

But definitely a witch outfit.

Witches had little control over the appearance of their hat and outfit. Their hat and outfit were part of their magic and connected too closely to their magical abilities. They struggled even to wear different outfits. Only minor changes at best worked.

Unless they suppressed their own magical abilities.

They could—but for only so long.

So Roo finally met with the eyes of this witch. Potentially his next target—or outright enemy right here and now.

If she was rearing to fight.

If.

CHAPTER 6
ROO DE BLADES

An if as big as that heavenly endowed ginormous chest of hers.

And those big eyes of hers ... glowing a brilliant azure blue with sparkling streaks of sky blue ... not actually enraged.

No.

Just annoyed. Typical waiting-too-long-on-line kind of annoyed.

For now.

That this pink-haired beauty choose to wait rather than cause trouble right away—a very good sign she didn't intend to cause trouble.

Least not here, at this town.

It's not like that towering high wall, its seaweed-choked moat, let alone its wobbly creaky drawbridge posed much of a threat to any real witch with any real power.

So what if her eyes now rolled dismissively annoyed at finally meeting his gaze?

Her pink cute lips grimaced?

She hadn't caused trouble yet.

In fact. Her dimpled cute cheeks. They were a touched flushed pink too. So good.

Awkward reaction. Not entirely one sided then.

So, of course, playing the love-struck womanizing bard his dad often, in fact, was, Roo bowed gracefully and apologically toward the erotically gorgeous pink-haired witch girl.

A girl who, as a witch, could sense whether he spoke the truth, so ...

"What gorgeous style!" Roo said. "What a heavenly endowed sight to behold! Apologies, m'lady, but—"

"Yeah, yeah 🩶" she said. "I've heard it **all** before 🩶"

She even huffed her stunningly colossal and near bare-naked chest out at Roo. As if testing him and his restraint not to ogle there, or worse.

So, of course, Roo gave her his most charming smile and wink.

"Ah, heart broken recently then," he said, "and wandering wide under the fair blue sky not helping, dreams of a big beautiful future together shattered forever and—"

Her cheeks flushed a bit more. Now more red than pink too.

"Oh no no no 💧" she said. "It's not like ... I ... I just never had a boyfriend before 💔"

Her gloved hands jerked off her hips and awkwardly

folded over each other on her amazingly smooth and bare-naked midriff.

Okay. Yeah.

Too many guys wouldn't believe her but yeah. It happened. All too often, in fact.

His dad wooed so many of them too.

Successfully.

Revealing to Roo just how often a truly stunningly gorgeous girl could end up struggling for dates, let alone more, since the guys she'd actually want to date were far too nervous and outright chicken-shit scared to even talk to her honestly (especially to a stunningly gorgeous witch. That whole sensing-the-truth thing striking hard here too) let alone actually ask her out on any kind of real date ...

"Most guys," she said, "are too scared of us witches to ever ... you know💔"

Ah. Least she realized it. Unlike some girls.

Some thought there was something wrong with them, or they were actually ugly, or some other crap.

Least according to dad—and to mom.

"I know, m'lady," Roo said. "So now's the best time to start! Name's Roo. Yours?"

The pink-haired witch girl actually perked up, and cheerfully too.

"I'm Juliet💔 " she said. "Juliet Heartequin💔 But my friends ..."

A sudden sad look came over her heavenly heart of a beautiful baby face?

"Your friends ..." Roo said, "something happen to them?"

"Yeah," Juliet said, "They ... they went—"

That's when Tinsel, still behind, and beside Roo to the left, huffed so loud and scornfully Juliet clearly felt intimidated. As intimidated as Tinsel clearly felt scorned and annoyed.

Her drawbridge and toll clearly still waited for him, and others.

"Of course, Bard Boy," Tinsel said. "That girl's a witch. A **powerful** witch. And those lousy witch friends of hers must have been taken down by Exorcists. Trapped in some lousy dungeon or worse. So leave before she turns you into a newt—or worse."

Sure the troublemaking monsters Exorcists captured often got tossed into special isolated dungeons but ...

But, whatever happened to her friends, even if her friends were other witches, Juliet here didn't seem like the enraged-to-war type. Eager to hate and hex and hurt others. Conquer or destroy humanity or whatever.

Least not yet. So ...

"And what a lucky newt I'd be!" Roo said. "To newt or to newt, *that* is the question."

That got him a cute little giggle from Juliet. She even fiddled a bit with her hot-pink hair, curling some of that hot-pink hair once curled around her ginormous right breast around and around her right forefinger.

"Wow🤍" Juliet said. He's actually not so bad. "Too bad I left my newting wand at home🤍"

Her cute little blush even spread down her neck, and to her shoulders even. Exactly the kind of blush dad induced in unexperienced beauties back a decade or so ago. Back when Roo was a teen even more eager for his own conquests in love and you know.

But, of course, Tinsel groaned. Sighing even more annoyed now.

Dad would have wooed both girls at once. Roo ... still could have learned more from him.

Especially for this kind of thing, here and now.

"Hey," Tinsel said, "Get a clue, you idiot."

But Roo knew better than to give up so quickly. Especially now. Juliet seemed more than interested and willing to play along—if not more. Plenty of witches—and other monsters—helped exorcists out, if they didn't become Exorcists themselves.

"Such jealousy!" Roo said. "No need to call this lovely witch names."

Tinsel grunted. "I meant *you*, Bard Boy."

Tinsel then grabbed his left hand. Tight and painfully secure. Too secure to escape—let alone call forth anything from the infinity glove on that hand.

Least his shawl's long sleeve still hid that Exorcist emblem on his glove.

Mostly.

"Don't you know," Tinsel said, "there's a war between monsters like her and humans like you. A world war. Not just here but **everywhere**. So—"

"There's a war now?" Roo said. "Excellent! Forbidden love is it! Right Juliet? The most exciting kind of love! Let's go for it and—"

Smack!

CHAPTER 7
ROO DE BLADES

The smack. It left. It left Roo reeling sideways.

The towering high wall. Tilted. Tilted as much sideways as he felt.

The moat too. Still except for the stray bubble bursting here or there.

And what looked like a few pairs of big bulging white eyes near the drawbridge. On both sides?

What the ,,,

And the drawbridge. Still creaky and rickety and far too fragile to handle a sudden sideways anything so ... ugh.

But Juliet. No. Not the culprit. She was shocked. Aghast. No.

Tinsel did it,

Tinsel had smacked the side of his head. Hard. Not deadly hard. Not skull lumping hard.

Just thought-breaking hard

And just as quickly—those white bulging eyes had vanished? What the ...

"Enough," Tinsel said, "**is** *enough*. No coin, no entry. Period. Now go. NOW!!!"

"Alas," Roo said. "Looks like I'll just have to—"

Tinsel growled. "Just what? Sing your way into the dungeon?"

But then Juliet gasped, again, brushing aside her lush wedges of hot-pink hair curled around her ginormous chest.

Staring shocked at Tinsel. Not at Roo.

"W-W-Wait 🤍" Juliet said. "I'll ... I'll pay for him 💘"

Tinsel tsked. Clearly even more angry now.

"So you two are together?" Tinsel said.

"Well ... I guess ..." Juliet said.

"Of course!" Roo said.

Smiling at how that sweetheart of a witch just saved him a butt load of trouble trying to climb the wall, or searching for another way inside.

Juliet gulped, all too loud and clear, but then nodded, smiling even more nervously.

"Okay," Juliet said, "Roo's with me, but ... is there ... is there really a war? *Now?* B-B-But ..."

"Exactly!" Tinsel said. "So surrender peacefully or else ..."

The next instant.

Quicker than a blink.

Than a thought.

Tinsel struck.

CHAPTER 8
ROO DE BLADES

It was over in an instant.

Quicker than a blink. A blink of an instant.

The cloudless blue sky still auraed the erotically gorgeous Juliet from behind. Making her whole entire outfit sparkle and glow like the magic it was.

The belt and its golden heart buckle around her ginormous chest. The utltrashort and ultrasnug skirt and its golden threaded flames along the bottom to the hot-pink along the top. Even her beret and its golden threaded flames along the bottom and the hot-pink on the rest of it.

Even her snazzy stylish shin boots.

Their hot-pink shiny leather. Their ruby-red heart. The golden chain laced them together.

The noon sun. Perfect for blazing down there on Juliet right there and then.

The moat only paces behind Roo. It then bubbled wet and smacked loud like far wet lips.

As if hint-hinting in its own way that he should aim for kissy kissy with Juliet as soon as he possible could.

Just like his dad would have directed him to.

Except a few clumps of sliced seaweed suddenly lay beside the drawbridge?

What the …

And the scent of Tinsel behind Roo. It mixed with the scent of Juliet before Roo. All into a nice rich candyish fruit salad of black cherries mixed with strawberries and vanilla.

Enough to get a guy's heart thumping for more.

More flirty fun from both gorgeous girls.

Despite his most urgent of missions to save Twin Pearl right here and now.

But Tinsel. Her left saber. The tip of its blade.

Already through that big hollow golden heart of the belt around Juliet's heavenly endowed ginormous chest.

Now. Already.

That tip was buried between Juliet's ginormously big breasts. A certain kill strike—if the blade sunk much deeper.

Tinsel smirked. "Your annoying seaweed monsters paid the price. Your turn now."

Just as Juliet jolted with a gasp. Freezing tenser then tense.

"B-B-But," Juliet said, "they weren't—ack!"

Juliet cringed in pain. "Okay, okay, I surrender💔 Please don't—Ouchie 🤍 Ouchie 🤍 Ouchie 🤍 I—ah, ah, ah … I didn't …"

Juliet. Her elbows suddenly hugging her near-bare-naked waist. Hands held up, by her shoulders. Palms shown and empty, except ... a pentagram of braided golden threads was woven into her fingerless gloves' hot-pink palms.

Infinity gloves. Infinity gloves were part of her witch outfit? Wow.

She wasn't just as witch, but a **powerful** witch.

One already in complete and utter surrender? Strange.

Enraged witches didn't usually act pull the innocent girlie card so quickly, not unless they really were innocent, usually.

Time to save his first witch of the day.

Since that blade—its shiny silver appearance.

Good.

Not black so not cold iron. Nope.

Cold iron wasn't a regular iron, no, but a special metal. It not only suppressed any and all magic by mere touch alone, it quickly drained monsters of their magic. All of it. The more cold iron touched the more it drained the magic away.

Same for any creature of magic. Not just monsters.

Like mermaids. Fairies.

Even elves.

Especially elves—or those with enough elven blood.

So, of course, Tinsel, playing the elf girl, would avoid wielding cold iron blades.

Her blades weren't bright blue either.

So they weren't cold steel either. (Sometimes called divine steel because it was as bright and blue as the sky itself.) Cold steel had a similar effect as cold iron but far more powerful and worse, scolding agony to the mere touch.

So Roo couldn't help but smile comfortingly at Juliet—to ease some of her obvious shock and growing worry.

"Woh, woh, woh, there Tinsel," Roo said. "No need to—ack!"

Tinsel. Her other saber. Her right saber.

Its tip then pressed against his own neck—despite wearing the hood of his shawl.

But his Exorcist uniform. Sure it would protect him against regular steel. Protect him better than even steel armor could. Assuming those blades weren't magical themselves.

If.

An if as big as Juliet's amazingly ginormous chest.

The sudden breeze. It rustled the freshly cut short grass.

Reminding Roo of his real purpose here too.

Stop the coming attack.

And Tinsel here might be intending just that. Stopping the attack. Even if she was definitely a monster of some sort too.

A regular elf girl guard would have, by now, already lost interest in him. His uniform, the magic woven throughout it, it should have deflected her interest, and lead her to forget him while he chatted up Juliet.

So Roo, as he raised his hands in complete and utter surrender, just like Juliet did.

He also barked out a laugh.

A genuine playful laugh.

"Hey Juliet," Roo said. "Looks like our scheme to steal all the candy in Twin Pearl hit a snag."

Juliet grimaced. "Speak for yourself🩶 I'm just warming up, he-he—ouchie❣️"

Tinsel scowled at them both. Her sabers. Unmoving.

And deadly serious.

"Enough," Tinsel said, "with the jokes, you two. My voice already rendered your magic moot, Witch Girl—"

Roo blinked. Smiling as friendly as he could, and as excited as he now felt.

No wonder he hadn't bothered to try to fight.

Good thing too.

Tinsel here might actually be some kind of witch too—and might not even be entirely aware of it, especially if she started out as another kind of monster, one that could hid her monster identity.

"A magical voice!" Roo said, "Perfect for a bard-to-be! Come with us and—"

Tinsel tsked. "To the dungeon? Ha! If you get out ... I might consider it. Maybe."

"You hear that Juliet?" Roo said. "We'll soon have our third member!"

Juliet giggled, smiling bright despite her obvious worry.

"Yup!" Juliet said. "We'll get all that candy yet!"

Tinsel growled, the huffed. Her gaze only directed at Roo now.

"Don't count your bandages before they mend, Bard Boy."

"Bandages?" Roo said. "Mend? Ha! That's a mummy saying. Wow excellent job shifting your bandages to that elven uniform—ack!"

Tinsel smacked the bottom of his jaw with the flat of her right saber.

And so quickly too—too quickly for Roo to react. Now with her magical voice clearly and obviously slowing him down.

"Enough!" Tinsel said. "Bud! Get out here and cuff this witch before she recovers her magic and tie up this awful bard boy too!"

Roo sighed. "Hit a nerve ... or should I say, ripped a bandage?"

The next smack from Tinsel left Roo dazed.

But seeing how happy Juliet looked ... worth the smacking.

Worth all the smacking Tinsel could dish out, and then some.

CHAPTER 9
TINSEL SPARKLES

Done and done with escorting two more prisoners in the town's dungeon but Tinselletta Sparkles still had to return to that awful post at the drawbridge for the rest of the day all because "reasons."

Captain Killjaw reasons.

So off to drawbridge guard duty once again.

Least the streets here, like most human settlements on hills and stuff, formed concentric circles. Seven of them—each with five equally spaced out streets connecting the concentric streets.

(Listening to tales here and there, human or monster, kinda sortof helped sometimes, with things like this.)

The streets themselves were barely wide enough for four really fat human guys standing shoulder to shoulder. Several paces wide of white smooth stone and yet the racket those four-wheeled wood wagons made racing around and around during the few hours at night they were still allowed to travel about ...

How did any of the humans here sleep at all?

Least none of these butt-ugly humans bothered to look her way anymore. No. They cleared their small streets whenever Tinsel or her remaining teammates showed up.

So returning to the gateway ...

Quicker than quick, even when she walked kinda sort of fast. Her boots clonking steadily against the hard stone road.

Echoing as sharp as her twin blades.

The next turn into the shady gateway tunnel and another few too many echoey steps and Tinsel was soon back at the drawbridge and ugh.

Those creaks, cracks, and splashes only moments ago—the drawbridge finally broke apart. Again. Falling a few feet into that stinky seaweed-choked moat.

Again.

Third time since dawn today and ... sigh.

Destroying that drawbridge the first time, the time a week or so ago when her whole entire team actually arrived, more like invaded this dump of a human settlement known as Twin Pearl.

Yeah, it so defs was a big mistake but stopping that weed-butt Bud and his buddy, that overly cocky Clem from being so super stupid competitive and ...

Harder than stopping a pair of drunk stupid flies from buzzing around, then right into the spider's web together.

Bad enough that weed-butt Bud got to shirk the rest of his guard duty onto Tinsel.

Sure, using gloves to carry the cold iron shackles, Bud cuffed that pink-haired witch girl Juliet what's-her-face in the blackest of cold iron cuffs—all so that her magic was suppressed completely, and yeah, Tinsel never ever wanted to touch cold iron ever again.

The last time. It really drained her dry quickly. Exhausted dry.

Why Bud didn't even bother binding the bard boy's hands, not even with the plain ordinary rope he had with him, since, of course, Bud insisted that bard boy Roo-whatever was far too harmless to waste any precious rope on.

As if rope was precious or rare or something.

That the bard boy took the whole capture thing so ... well. Amazingly well. Weirdly well.

Enough that Juliet clearly played along as well too. Staying calm and reframed from the usual threats or cries for mercy or whatever.

Tinsel couldn't help but kinda sortof like them both for it.

Even if that bard boy had snubbed Tinsel for that Juliet and so quickly too, all while at that awful break-happy draw-bridge ... well.

Roo even thanked her for her hard work. No hard feelings over this misunderstanding.

Juliet then did the same silly thing.

Weirdos.

But nice weirdos. Almost enough ... some guilt throwing them in the dungeon but ... sigh.

That bard boy. Far too smooth for a girl's good. Smoother than a ... a ... sigh.

The stone here. So smooth.

But that bard boy.

Even smoother.

Yeah.

That smooth. Winning over that powerful witch Juliet so quickly too ...

Maybe Tinsel had been too hard on him but ... that witch ... orders **were** orders, and ... little chance that bard boy actually knew her.

But that so-called renegade faction of witches known as Hellion Hexists ....all crazy powerful witches, supposedly ... all intent on conquering all the other monsters factions, and human factions ... ugh.

If humanity and their Exorcists weren't bad enough trouble.

This wide moat and its thick seaweed was almost as much trouble. No line of butt-ugly humans to ogle her but she couldn't just go back in defeat. Not without getting scolded by the captain. Maybe getting worse duties thrown at her—or thrown in the dungeon herself.

What to do ... what to do ...

CHAPTER 10
ROO DE BLADES

As far as dungeons go, Twin Pearl's wasn't half bad. Pretty nice, actually.

The drafts through these blackest of cold iron bars, just like the line of those bars through the rectangular oak frame of this solid secure door, they were only mildly warm.

Not chilly cold. Not at all bone-chillingly cold like some dungeons. Let alone baking-oven hot like other dungeons.

Nope.

Pretty comfy, actually.

These vertical bars speared through the few-inch-thick frame of solid dark oak, since, of course, a solid whole door would give prisoners far too much precious privacy here.

And the space between the bars. Less than a couple few inches wide. Barely enough to squeeze his fingers between them. Barely. The bars themselves. An inch or so thick and smoothly round.

Not rough. Not rough at all.

Not as smooth as dad wooing a lovely lady. More like as smooth as Roo doing so.

Yeah.

More like Roo smooth.

But still, pretty comfy.

Well, as long as you weren't a monster, or monster-blooded, since cold iron suppressed any and all magic by mere touch alone. It also quickly drained monsters of their magic. All of it. The more cold iron touched the more it drained the magic away.

So shackling monsters with it—a quick and simple way to keep them helpless.

But ... same for any creature of magic. Not just monsters.

So not Roo.

So no worries brushing the bars. Grabbing them. Or anything.

Like waving good-bye like a cheerful appreciative idiot at Bud back after Bud threw both Roo and Juliet in here, and then strutted away, back down the hallway.

Thankfully Bud embraced his inner elf and looked down at Juliet as well as Roo.

That whole humans of any sort, mundane or magical, were butt ugly you knows.

(Even humans turned into witches.)

That Bud. He was normally a very corruptible, but also a very bribable vampire-posing-as-an-elf-stud. That handsome blonde stud of a pale-faced vampire also owed Roo several times over for ... what some might call ... help, yes, help in the past, over the last few many years.

As in owed butt loads of coin **and** favors to Roo.

So yeah, good thing Bud didn't recognized him, yet—or else he'd so try and insist on helping Roo, all to reduce the amount of coin and favors owed to Roo.

Big time.

Better let everyone—including Bud for the moment—continue to think Roo was a harmless fool of a bard boy, for now.

The smell of the dungeon here, carried by the draft into his face, wasn't half bad either.

Cold iron often smelled not just irony but salty too. Like salt-filled iron. As in the kind of powder some lunatics used against lesser monsters, and it actually, sometimes worked too.

This cozy block of a cell here, the narrow hallway it was connected to, even the wall a couple paces across from the cell, all just the usual musty stone whatever. No awful stenches of the unspeakable kind that were common among more mundane dungeons.

No strange mysterious whatever stinks either.

Just plain good old musty stone—touched nicely with fragrant old but quality oak. White stone everywhere. The stone itself was nothing to write home about—if he had a home to write to, that was, and headquarters didn't count—but the sheered sleek and smooth stone wasn't awfully rough or dirty in any real way either.

Just regular clean white stone. As smooth as dad wooing another lovely lady.

If only Crooster could see Roo now. Hopefully that shapeshifting crow would find him soon. The magical contract between them wasn't actually a familiar contract, so no, it didn't link them together in such a way that Crooster could find Roo easily through the contracted bond.

Still. That crow would find Roo.

He always did.

For now, even better, Roo and Juliet now had this whole entire block of cells all to their very selves. So, least for now, no moans and whines and whimperings.

Except their own—once they reached that point. If they reached that point.

If.

CHAPTER 11
RŒO DE BLADES

An if as big as Juliet's heavenly-endowed ginormous chest.

Not even Juliet reached that point ... yet.

Good.

And she was definitely a newbie at this whole dungeon prisoner thing.

Even with her hands cuffed hopelessly snug in inch-thick cuffs of cold iron and, worse, cuffs chained together with several inches of inch-thick links, as if she really was a truly terrifying danger.

But no. Juliet was taking this whole thing better than expected.

A lot better.

Even with her a pace or two in front of him, and another pace to his left side.

Not that there was much space to his right. Almost none before the white stone wall.

And even less between Juliet and that small square barred window in the center of the wall opposite of the barred doorway. A window Juliet clearly couldn't help but keep glancing out of.

Even if it was only to another white stone wall a few dozen paces away.

And above them ... a barred view of the sky. Thankfully a cloudless sky today. No protection from the rain here, or the other elements. Nope. So things could be worse. A lot worse. Just a nice blazing hot noon...ish sun.

So yeah. Julet doing a lot better than expected.

Even with a sad little smile over her pretty pink lips. A sad smile that somehow reached those brilliantly glowing blue eyes of hers. Big glowingly bright azure blues with sparkling streaks of sky blue.

A stray friendly glance or two his way every so often too.

Like just now. Another glance.

"Sorry about this💔" Juliet said. "I ... I didn't mean to drag you into my problems💔"

Oh wow no. She thought she was to blame for this mess?

Her hot-pink hair blocked some of the next glance, but he caught what mattered.

The sincerely of her shame.

So Roo gave Juliet the kind of graceful playful bow only a true bard could manage.

"No need to apologize," Roo said. "Now I have a roof over

my head and lovely company to spend time with. Our date is only just beginning!"

Her sad little giggle ...

"More disaster," Juliet said, "than date💔 So ... now what?"

Juliet just stood there, leaning gorgeously near-naked against the wall.

Her amazingly fine ass pressed against that white stone wall. Her ultrashort skirt of hot-pink and gold flames along the bottom, it now showed off even more stunningly sexy thigh and ruby-red panties underneath that couple-inch long skirt of sexy snugness.

So gulp was sexy distractingly right. Saving her somehow. A priority right now.

Despite the coming attack.

Since especially with the war nowadays—saving innocent monsters, that was just as important as stopping violent monsters—but rarely as glamorous, rarely paid well too, but still ...

Sigh. Duty was duty. Right was right.

Dad and mom were very clear on the difference between them and so on and so forth.

Her lush legs still leaned back. Her torso still leaned forward.

Some.

Juliet then rocked herself on the backs of her shin boots. Back and forth, back and forth. Rocking along the bottom of her low heels.

Just passing the time.

While scratching up the white stone floor up nice and loudly. Scratches that echoed sharp and loudly throughout the cell and then down the hallway, to both the left and right of their cell, and eventually faded away, no hint of another door closing them off from the outside.

And that movement of hers, it clearly helped ease her some. Keep her calm. Patient.

Even as, with each rocking motion, those inch-big ruby-red hearts down those boot sleeves chingled along with their golden chain laces.

Chingles that echoed eerily around the whole entire cell room. Down the hallway left and right.

And back to their cell here.

Unlike the scratches ... strange.

Very strange.

Which meant the hallway was sealed shut in some way—and not by a regular door or anything like that.

Through a spell or magic of some sort.

Or an unusual kind of monster ability.

CHAPTER 12
TINSEL SPARKLES

Sure normally the magic in her voice, her song would be strong enough to repair the drawbridge.

Just like Tinsel did so two times earlier today.

But there was only so much magic left in her after losing so many of her bandages. And there was no sign of any of the planks either. None. Just dark water and the seaweed choking the water dark green.

And defs not enough magic left to find the planks using her song and then repair the drawbridge using more of her song ...

If only that weed butt Bud would put the drawbridge back together this time too. But he already got out of the rest of his shift today. Captain always let Bud off easy. Making Tinsel take on his duty for today since vampires and the sun and stuff.

Lazy jerks!

Maybe she should take up that bard boy up on his offer.

Maybe ... if they escaped ... maybe she would.

Maybe.

Tinsel wasn't the only one who had to worry if any Exorcists of any order got into town.

The light shade underneath the gateway, within this echoey tunnel, even so close to the moat, it should be good enough to shield that weed butt plenty—or just have Clem do it. He was so brawny tall, even for a werewolf posing as an elf, the moat was more like a puddle to him.

A hard-to-trudge-through puddle.

Sun sucking down Bud and his vampire powers too low her ass. She wasn't even a vampire, just like that bard boy figured out, Tinsel was a mummy, an eighteen-year-old mummy, an elven mummy just barely old enough to be stuck serving in this crazy crapola war of idiots against other idiots.

Even this eighteen-year-old mummy girl knew that moat wasn't running water, so no worries about it weakening Bud and his vampire powers even more than the sun already did, nope, not at all, so there.

But of course captain insisted that Tinsel give Bud half of her bandages.

Half.

Then, of course, she shifted her remaining bandages into this snazzy elven-style guard uniform (minus any emblems, since no telling which idiots used what emblems.)

All on their captain's ... "request."

More like volunteered to give her precious bandages to Bud to "borrow," (the never-return kind of borrow.) She then had to mold those bandages into an elven-style uniform for him. One that would protect him from the sun and running water and stuff.

Including Exorcist crap that Tinsel, now, was way defs more vulnerable to.

But no saying no to Captain Killjaw.

The way that dragon-posing-as-an-elf captain of hers blabbered on and on about munching more and more "young maidens" exactly like Tinsel here ... so super **shudder**.

(No wonder so many humans avoid the whole lot of them.)

But now ... weird, weird how there was no line of humans beyond the moat. Still. Long after she returned. No sign of a single human anywhere there, or near here. All gone. Why ...

Still no sign of the drawbridge or its planks either. What the ...

Did ... did the humans steal the planks? Steal and run off with them? How ...

The moat was outright impassable with all that thick seaweed. It was up to Clem's waist. Deeper than any of those humans were tall so they'd have to swim and there was no hope of swimming through that seaweed.

Non at all.

So Tinsel. She.

She gnashed her teeth. "What in the ..."

Least she was allowed to carry, to use these twin steel blades. Common steel but high quality. Dwarf forged quality. Thanks to her dad slaying more than a few dwarves back in his day.

Since it's not like any of her bandages would grow back that quickly either.

Unlike vampires or werewolves whose body could regenerate limbs within moments—as long as they had the strength to or drained enough blood or whatever—it would take more than a few days for her bandages to restore themselves.

Maybe another week or so.

Even if she dunked, fed all her bandages a bucket of fresh human blood.

No chance she could find any human volunteers in town, let alone enough volunteers ... and forcing them ... ugh.

Not her style.

Sure, as a young mummy, she too could regenerate lost limbs—but only as long as she didn't lose too much of her bandages. Didn't drain too much of the magic stored with her bandages.

And right now her bandages were running as dry, as empty as—

The moat. Bubbles sudden surfaced. Popped loud and gooey clear.

Creepy clear.

Smelling like old farts? What the ... since when did those bubbles stink so badly?

Then.

That instant.

Her training in the sword. All the years of training her dad gave her.

She sang to herself. Pure instinct. All her remaining magic

into that song. Slowing down everyone, everything around her.

Everything except herself.

Speeding herself up several times. Several many times and —ack!

Her arm!

Her left arm was gone!

Gone from the shoulder down.

What the ... what ... what attacked her? What ... how. That speed. Too fast to see.

Too fast to even notice—until the attack was done.

Her elven uniform. No stopping it. It dissolved back into bandages.

Each bandage was as wide as her palm. A few inches wide. A light tan fabric similar to very finely combed wool. Some wrapped around her hips. Some around her chest.

Both kinda loosely but staying in place because of their magical nature.

And her instinctive modesty—as mom warned her— should keep her bandages from falling off completely, revealing too much, no matter how skimpy little remained.

Enough remained to cover the wound. Stop it from bleeding her out. But ... what.

No.

Tinsel.

She turned. Turned toward the street opposite of the moat.

And dashed out of there.

Away from that evil smelly moat. Away from whatever

attacked her. It must have come from that moat. Something worse than those seaweed monster things before. Those stinky bubbles. A warning.

So get away from that moat. Get away from it as fast as she could.

Through the tunnel. The gateway tunnel. It was only a few several sprints to the street cutting through it. So a turn or two soon and she'd be safe.

Safe enough ...

Only her huffing breath echoed in the tunnel.

Echoed and echoed.

Her aching legs. Her bare aching feet pounding the stone harder and harder.

No bandages left on her other than over her chest and hips now.

None.

So magic. Low. Far too low.

Her legs. They sprinted as fast as she could. Wind gusting around her. Warm and yet chilly. Too chilly too suddenly.

So Tinsel. She sang for her life. Singing to slow down whatever was coming for—ack!

Her right arm!

Gone!

Gone from the shoulder down!

No!

No!

No!

Her singing. Why wasn't it working? Why wasn't it slowing that thing down?

What was it?

What was eating her?

What the ...

Tinsel dashed faster and faster. Down to the white stone street. It shouldn't be taking this long. She should have reached the street at the end by—

CHAPTER 13
ROO DE BLADES

Even stuck in this small cozy comfy block of a white stone cell.

Even with the noon sun blazing down through the wide barred window above them..

Even with no obvious escape unless Roo revealed his true identity—that he was an Exorcist, which might ruin whatever was happening between Juliet and himself.

But hiding it for too long ... just as bad.

If not worse.

So, of course, to delay the inevitable, Roo couldn't help but glance down at those soles of her snazzy hot-pink shin boots.

At the golden glimmer from them as she wobbled on her feet. At the brilliant but stunningly clean dark-pink soles a couple few inches thick and woh, even more surprising, another set of hollow golden hearts were solidly embedded in the soles of each boot.

Meaning her movements might probably be boosted by her own magic somehow.

Roo gulped. Returning her sad smile.

No shackles on him. No obvious restraints. Not even simple rope.

Nothing. Thanks to Bud actually.

Tinsel had so wanted to restrain him too, but Bud over-ruled her, and so callously too.

No wonder Tinsel left them in such a foul mode.

But Roo's infinity gloves had exactly what he needed to break out. Even with his elven partner missing in action he still had his second best blade. An inanimate but magical blade that could deflect, and cut magic, but only after absorbing enough magic beforehand.

It also could double as either a solid short sword or a whip of short interconnected blades.

So breaking down that door. Or any of the walls ...

He could.

If he put enough strength behind the blows using that second blade, the whip blade. Assuming no cold iron bars were ledge withing the walls or floor. A big id. Bigger than Juliet's ginormous chest.

Sure his training let him boost what his regular strength could do several times over but against solid cold iron bars rein-forcing the stone, if they were there and reinforcing the stone?

Maybe.

Only maybe.

And they'd be needed to store any monsters here for any length of time—especially if the shackles proved less effective than expected.

So yeah. Bars probably reinforced the stone. Hidden within the stone.

So how to reveal himself as an Exorcist to Juliet without frightening her? Making her panic?

Better do it soon. Before worse trouble strikes.

And it was coming sooner than he expected.

Especially with that inhumanly natural-looking hot-pink hair of hers flowing straight down and over her nearly bare shoulder blades. Humans didn't have hot-pink hair naturally. And Roo could tell dyed hair from natural hair, thanks to mom and dad and their ... unintentional training in ... certain areas.

Elf-blooded people could have naturally unusual hair colors too. Any from the rainbow.

And beyond.

Some monsters could. Especially witches.

Even dragons shifted into their human form.

Especially dragons that did more than shift into a human form, but awakened as witches.

And that unique witch hat of hers, her snazzy beret of hot-pink with golden flames along the base.

Just what was the nature of her magic?

Of course, as a witch, her magic helped her maintain her appearance—after all her appearance also reflected the extent of her magic and its potency, especially her dress and hat, at least to some degree.

Maybe that strawberries and vanilla candy-like smell was connected to her magic? That smell had weakened ever since she was cuffed in cold iron shackles.

But the smell hadn't vanished. Not entirely.

As if it was part of her magic, not just some candy she had been chewing.

So no wonder her wonderfully stylish wedges of hot-pink hair still curled sexy cute around that ginormous chest of hers, a heavenly-endowed chest still strapped snuggly in that hot-pink belt and its hollow heart of gold buckle over the center of her chest.

A chest he did his best not to leer too obviously at.

Except her fingers. Both left and right forefingers. They now nervously twirled the ends of her hot-pink wedges of hair. Staying nicely near to her heavenly-endowed ginormous and near-naked breasts.

But his dad. He wouldn't have hesitated. Think to much about what he'd need to do.

He'd just do it.

Woo Juliet over as a lover—and maybe, even more.

"'Now what?', you say ..." Roo said.

And Roo strolled calmly, and confidently over to Juliet. Since girls—human or monster—tended to fall for confident calm guys like guys tended to fall for girls with a good pair of tits and ass on an hourglass-to-heaven body.

So Roo slipped his hands under hers. Holding them nice and gently.

Careful not to let the emblem on the back of his gloves slip beyond his droopy sleeves. Not yet,, that was, but soon he would.

Soon.

Juliet gulped loud and nervously clear.

"Heeey♥" Juliet said. "Roo? Are you ... are you really just a bard?"

"Hay is for horses," Roo said, "and I'll be your stallion."

Juliet giggled again.

But her shoulders stayed up and tight. In a tense shrug.

"Oh yeah?" Juliet said. "Then ... tell me ... Stallion Boy, who are you really? What's your *real* name?"

"That's easy," Roo said. "Too easy. Romeo de Blades. But everyone just calls me Roo."

"And?" Juliet said.

Roo huffed a little smile. Clever girl.

More like clever witch. That whole honest truth sensing thing again. She clearly sensed just how much he left out. Not lied. Not actually.

But just left out.

Her hands squeezed in his hands back gently.

"Please?" Juliet said. "We're ... we're friends, right?"

Yeah.

Roo chuckled to himself, just like dad would have at this moment.

That whole honest truth thing made flirting, teasing her silly much harder than it should be—or comforting a witch, especially without a single white lie.

"More than friends!" he said. "Lovers to be if—"

"*If* you tell me the truth," Juliet said, "I'll ... I'll let you do lover ... stuff to me, okay?"

Uh huh. Lover stuff. Yeah.

Definitely not as experienced as she looked. Good but ... awkward way to say that but yeah.

Definitely taking her up on that offer.

"Careful there," Roo said, "I just might take you up on that offer."

"You better 🤍 🤍 🤍" Juliet said. "You're ... more than bard, aren't you? A bard and a ..."

Another gentle squeeze of his hands. Clearly waiting, hoping for him to confirm her suspicion. Whatever her suspicion was.

Probably she already suspected the truth.

"And if I am ..." Roo said, "a ... you know ..."

Juliet smirked. A twinkle in her eyes. Looking him down and over once again.

"Then ... you know," Juliet said, "there's something hidden under that shawl, isn't there?"

The moment Roo cocked his head sideways ...

The moment she throw another sudden naughty little smirk his way.

"Something naughty?" Juliet said, "or something ... pervy? Or ... let me see, okay? It can't be more pervy than what I'm wearing, right?"

So Roo barked out a laugh.

"You've got a dirty mind," Roo said, "for an innocent witch."

"Maybe I'm not so innocent😼 " Juliet said, "Just … inexperienced, that's all🤍 You can help me … fix that, right?"

Oh wow yes.

Juliet was clearly on a roll so Roo let her ramble on.

"Just tell me the truth first and then … he-he, we **are** alone, after all …"

Roo couldn't help but give her a naughty smirk back.

So he looked straight into her eyes. Those big glowingly brilliant azure-blue eyes with their mesmerizingly sparkling sky-blue streaks. One of the more lovelier signs of her monster nature.

"Alright," Roo said. "Just promise not to panic."

Juliet huffed pouty at him. "I'll panic all I want, thank you very much🤍"

But that cutesy sweet smirk of hers didn't go away either.

So yeah. Time to reveal he was an Exorcist. Reveal it before she found out another way.

A less … better way.

CHAPTER 14
TINSEL SPARKLES

Tinsel. She.

She was alive?

But ... but where ... where was she?

The white stone all above her ... so shadowy light gray. Who knew how far above her it was? Too far to care. Since her back. Already laying against hard and smooth and really warm something ... more stone?

Maybe. Probably. If she was still in Twin Pearl ... everything was defs stone.

Gooey bubbles popped even more gooey loud and awful paces above her head.

The stink of old farts then ... then the sound of ugly lips smacking themselves loud and watery icky. The stink of fresh seaweed and newly cut grass and ... oh no. Only that awful moat in Twin Pearl stank like that. The grass ... only the dirt and grass around the hill smelled like that right outside of Twin Pearl.

And the warm breeze ... it tickled her from her toes to her nose.

What the ... was Tinsel, was she still in the gateway's tunnel? Laying there. On the stone floor?

But how? Why? What happened to her?

She was certain ... certain she had died by ... by something mysterious but .. awful and ...

A crow cawed all-too-loudly by the top of her head.

Hopped onto her forehead. Its tiny talons dug into her skin and skull for a moment.

Until it hopped over to her chest. The hand-sized bird with what looked like a crimson eyepatch over its left eye. An eyepatch with two concentric circles overlapping a thick cross.

That emblem ... where had she heard of it, seen it before?

The crow perched itself on the last of her bandages, the one hanging between her breasts, the only one left giving her the slightest bit of privacy there.

Facing her, looking down at her face, the crow cawed again. Then spoke?

Spoke as clear as any butt-ugly human, but with a birdy cawish voice.

"*Niiice* pigtails," the crow said. "Almost as nice as your tits here, mummy girl."

Tinsel tried to slap the perverted crow off her chest but ... her arms, they wouldn't, wouldn't move. In fact. They barely budged at all. Just twitched. Slightly.

Not from constraints, nopsies, but from being too tired, too weak to move?

What the …

All she could do was moan like some half-dead and delusional idiot.

A moan that echoed far too loudly through what had to be that gateway's stupidly tall tunnel. That there were no humans making noise nearby either … just silence … except for the breeze rustling the nearby grass over the hilltop and the stray watery fart of a bursting bubble in that awful seaweed-choked moat …

The crow cawed again.

"Ha!" the crow said. "Still recovering. Next time, Sweet Tits, run **away** from the dangerous monster—*not* toward it."

Uh huh. Scolded by a perverted crow. What was next …

But then again, even her dad used to like to testing her like this, occasionally, at least, and he'd always use a perverted familiar of course, all to make sure she didn't get too "attached to her modesty" and "rely too much on her girlie charm" and whatever.

A gulp and Tinsel finally managed more than a moan. More like a croak. A few words.

Prove she wasn't a complete idiot.

Just a big stupid one.

"So the price," Tinsel said, "what's the price for saving me? Getting this second chance."

The crow cawed happy again. Bouncing slightly on her bandage hanging across her breasts.

"Good!" the crow said, "Maybe you're just naive, not stupid."

Tinsel grimaced. Still. So weak that. That even grimacing took a lot of effort. Still.

Worth it.

Kinda.

"Can't have my other ... companion," the crow said, "fall for the wrong tits and ass."

Uh huh ...

"So ..." Tinsel said, "I'm the right tits and ass ... for who exactly?"

"Oh, no worries," the crow said, "you know him as Bard Boy."

"Bard Boy?" Tinsel said. "Oh ... *great*. So that Juliet's the wrong tits and ass? Maybe dying ... not as bad."

Tinsel competing for Bard Boy with that Juliet? Ughies.

No question Juliet defs won that war, completely, and that naive idiot probably didn't even realize the fight had even happened between them over that stupid boy.

"Ha!" the crow said. "Almost funny there. Almost. But no. I don't mean Juliet."

"Then ... who?" Tinsel said.

"You realize," the crow said, "the next part of dying from that monster before ... getting digested live, awake, and screaming in utter awful agony since well, that agony and suffering is what that familiar feeds off of, mostly."

"Familiar?" Tinsel said. "So a witch ... got me, before?"

"Yup!" the crow said, "More like her evil familiar. So time

to repay that favor you owe me by—oh don't try to get up yet. I'm not stupid enough to let you finish recovering much yet."

This crow ... what was he really? But asking him outright ... yeah, like that would work.

Tinsel tsked. Heart sinking deeper and ickier than a stone in that awful farting moat.

"Okay, okay," Tinsel said, "what do I need to do?"

"Go spellblade," the crow said, "as a familiar for Bard Boy, and quickly. Just agree to it and I'll do the rest right here and now. Then—"

"A spellblade?" Tinsel said. "But I wasn't born able to shift into a sword!"

"So?" the crow said. "Shifting into a singing sword—"

"Even if you make me into one ..." Tinsel said, "how ... how do I ..."

"I'll take care of it," the crow said. "Instinct. You'll know enough to get by. Then—"

"Then what?" Tinsel said. "Be that lout's heart broken—"

"Better a broken heart," the crow said, "then one wasted on nothing."

"Oh yay," Tinsel said, "time to be another wannabe bard girl ..."

"Oh," the crow said, "it won't be *that* bad. More annoying than bad. Probably."

"Uh huh, probably," Tinsel said, "but better a busty spellblade than a busted corpse."

But Bard Boy could then use her singing ability as his own, least while wielding her as a sword, through her, as a sword.

"Exactly!" the crow said. "So ... hurry up and agree."

"Okay, okay," Tinsel said, "Guess negotiating terms isn't an option, right?"

"Right," the crow said, "no time anyway. Bard Boy's in bigger danger than he realizes. He dies and you ... forget this second chance, at the very least."

"Figures," Tinsel said. "Okay. I agree. It's not like I have any better options."

"Exactly!" the crow said, "now here's what you need to do once the painfully sparkling stars vanish."

"Painfully sparkling stars?" Tinsel said. "Oh no. I—"

"No more time for more chit chat," the crow said. "Ready for your next mission?"

Tinsel tsked—before twinkling stars suddenly flooded her vision and the pain.

Her sudden scream.

Silent.

Since the pain ... nearly too much to even scream from.

CHAPTER 15

RŒ DE BLADES

Yet Roo. He still hesitated.

His hackles. Screaming at him. Screaming at him to hold on. Wait a moment.

But why?

Juliet. Her voice echoed loud and clear down the hallway connected to the cell. Down left and right.

But those echoes vanished a few too many echoes early.

Even earlier than before.

And Juliet clearly hadn't noticed. Not yet. Maybe won't at all.

Until it was too late.

Especially when Juliet suddenly got all bouncy excited in place. Her hands still holding his, and still gently too.

"You're more than a bard, are you, Roo?" Juliet said. "You're ... well ..."

Oh no. Those echoes. Ending sooner and sooner.

So he needed to hear them.

And clearly.

"Okay, okay," Juliet said, "you don't **have** to tell me … friends respect each others secrets, right?"

Roo nodded. "But …"

So he took a deep calming breath—as quietly and unnoticeably as he could.

And wow, did Juliet and her cloud of strawberry and vanilla candy scent send him to heaven and back.

Juliet, after all, did offer to cover the toll for him. Offered to help him out—despite being complete strangers, even if that seemed to have gotten him lumped in with her own troubles too now.

And those echoes. Ending even sooner now. Far too much sooner.

Dangerously close sooner.

Nearing-the-door-to-their-cell soon. Only-paces-away-from-their-door soon.

So Roo kissed Juliet right there and then.

Her sweet pink lips. Wow. Quieted her right there and then.

Warm and moist lips and woh, the echoes of her voice, when he suddenly cut the source off through this passionate kiss, those echoes all vanished instantly, at once, leaving the whole place eerily silent.

Someone, or something else was there, nearby, and likely not a friendly something.

CHAPTER 16
ROO DE BLADES

Holding the hands of Juliet as tenderly as Roo could, her shock so obvious as she jolted ever so slightly in place the moment the kiss started.

Rattling the chains connecting her cuffs.

The rattles now echoing only throughout their cell—through their barred cell door—and vanishing there.

No a hint of noise from outside either.

Despite their barred but open ceiling. Their barred but open window.

Stranger and stranger.

Her wrists so close to each other. Rattling chains now getting extra heavy? What the .. that shouldn't happen. Magic shouldn't effect them at all. But they got heavier and heavier, despite how she obviously pressed them against her flat-toned tummy.

Even as she gripped his hands tighter and tighter.

Just like he started gripping hers tighter and tighter.

Unless her strength, it was fading too, and the weight of the shackles were kicking in.

Roo, his heart, it thumped far too hard, too fast, too stunningly delighted to let him hear what he needed to hear. Determine how quickly, how suddenly those rattle sounds, their sharp echoes, how they vanished near the cell door.

Or even within the cell itself.

As if dying was better than interrupting this crazy cute kiss.

Just the thought. The room. Warmer than before.

From embarrassment.

Pure wonderful embarrassment. Like he was a young nervous kidlet kissing his first girl once again. As naive as she was. As inexperienced.

And just as exciting.

The silent hallway. Merely paces to his left. Beyond the barred frame of oak.

Might as well be miles away.

The small window to the right. Its gentle weak but hot breeze.

Nothing compared to the heat of this kiss between Roo and Juliet.

Especially when Juliet. She breathed out slowly and steadily. Washing his face slow and steadily with that warm, that mysterious strawberries and vanilla scent of hers. Moaning ever so cutesy sweet as she did so. As if shocked as how wonderful this first kiss of theirs was.

Even when her snazzy shin boots. Their low heels. They scratched the floor extra loud and wiggling clear.

No echoes. None.

Not anymore.

Despite how the small stone room. How it was once full of echoes. From nearly each and every sound. Thanks to its stone walls.

His heart. Pounding so fast. So hard.

Her cuffs. Their chains. Suddenly so crazy heavy.

So matter how much she gripped his hands tighter and tighter.

He gripped hers tighter and tighter. Helped hold them up. Up against her toned tummy.

Her hands. They shivered faster and faster from strain.

Her hands, his hands, they both drooped more and more?

The hackles. The back of his neck.

Screaming.

Screaming a warning.

The attack.

It was coming.

Now.

And his hands. Held too tight. Far too tight.

Juliet. Her eyes. As closed tight. As tight as her grip on his hands.

Even now.

Slipping slowly. Her hands. Too heavy. Too heavy from the cuffs.

Her magic. It was definitely nearly drained away. Not just sealed. Vanishing along with her strength.

But not by enough.

He couldn't summon a weapon. His second best blade. Not yet. Not while she clung to tight to his hands.

No.

Not unless ...

All or nothing. No holding back. No doubt.

His fingers. All of them

He jerked them free. All but his thumbs. Thumbs she clung to. As if for dear life.

Until he pressed the back of all his fingers against her amazingly stunningly soft and warm waist of hers. The bottom of her tummy.

Let the weight of her hands, her cuffs, slip all his fingers down.

Down under her ultrasnug skirt. Her hollow heart of gold for a buckle.

Her jolts.

Extra shocked this time.

Her moan.

Extra squeaky.

She even wiggled her hips? Wiggled a little. Against the stone wall. Scrapping it even more,

Then more and more wiggles. Scraps.

Scraps without a single echo.

Then, suddenly ... no.

No sound from her ass against the stone wall?

Even she she wiggled sensually sexy. Wiggling to help slide her skirt down.

Slip down more and more.

Till they hung snuggly over her upper thighs.

His fingers down. Down over and fondling her finest most private of regions.

Regions hairless and heart-thumpingly smooth and warm and ... woh.

Scaled?

Yeah.

Sleek and stunningly smooth scales.

Not skin.

Not hair.

Pubic scales? Not pubic hair. Not even just skin.

Pubic scales?!

Was she ... yes, she was. Juliet was really a dragon. A dragon shifter awakened as a witch!

Her sudden gasp.

Her sudden jolt—just as his fingers slipped gently between her legs, between her thighs, and her grip.

She let go.

That instant.

Despite his pounding heart screaming to go on.

Despite every fiber of his being diving him forward. Forward to undress this wet dream of a dream girl.

To die. Die in blissful heart rather than react. React to save them both.

Roo. He. He couldn't. Couldn't yank his hands away from their blissful heaven. Not now.

Not yet.

Even when an even hotter silent breath slimed down onto the back of his neck.

Even when—

A caw. A familiar caw exploded his world above him. From the barred ceiling of the cell.

"Interrupting something?" Crooster said.

CHAPTER 17
ROO DE BLADES

That instant. That moment.

Clarity struck Roo.

Struck him harder than any smack by his elven partner who was shamefully far too late.

Even with the gorgeously pink-haired Juliet before him. Her shocked gasp as his hands jerked away from her privies. Her stunningly wonderful strawberries and vanilla candy scent, as weak as it had become, was still going strong enough to intoxicate him stupidly drunk with lust for her.

His eyes. Jerked open.

Same time as Juliet jerked hers open and woh.

No whites in hers. And slitted vertical pupils. Serpent-style dragon eyes.

The real eyes of a dragon shifter..

Just as hot breath slimed the back of his neck. Freezing his body for another moment.

And Juliet. Her eyes. Widened with terror. Vertical slitted pupils going even more slitted.

Slitted with utter fear.

"Oh Roo ..." Juliet said, "I'm **so** sorry ... I ..."

Crooster caw again. "Catch! And quickly!"

Just as the lovely lyrical voice of a sweet-voiced girl, kinda like Tinsel actually, started humming above him.

Paces right above him. By the bars of the ceiling.

Till the humming whatever started falling.

So Roo raised his right hand.

A humming weapon? Form Crooster?

Awesome!

So Roo caught the blade as it fell—blade somehow humming loud and clear.

CHAPTER 18

ROO DE BLADES

"No worries, Juliet," Roo said. "I'll save us both. I swear to. As an Exorcist of the Crimson Order."

No point hiding the truth now. Now it was time to save them. Save them all.

Thanks to Crooster.

And this new blade. Humming blade. It was a stunningly lightweight blade of some sort. Singing a hum even louder now. Very much like Tinsel—if she was here singing as that blade rather than guarding the drawbridge.

Its voice—or her voice—the sound echoed loud and clear through the cell.

Through the hallway connected to the cell. Both left and right.

Echoed and echoed till it faded away.

So that hum, it somehow countered whatever the attacker was doing.

Good.

Roo's turn too—

Juliet gasped. Right before him. Even more terrified. Cringing mere inches from him.

Cringing even more now.

"You...you're," Juliet said, "an Exorcist?! B-B-But ... please ♥ Please don't slave me ♥"

She even flinched so hard, eyes suddenly so drastically shut, her heavy shackles flew back up near her ginormous chest, before falling back down, and then, Juliet yelped, yelped as loud as the rattles of her shackles, when the shackles yanked her down several inches even more.

A rumbling low bestial growl erupted right behind Roo and his head.

"Slave? *No.* Familiar. **Yes!**"

Of course! Juliet here was a dragon. Powerful in her own right—with or without magic.

(When she wasn't shackled, of course.)

And as a dragon shifter, especially as a dragon shifter witch, she could be, and so many would seek to forcefully familiar her. Another witch. Other monsters.

Even by some less ... honorable Exorcists.

Roo. He tried to turn. But his feet. Stuck to the stone floor? As if engulfed in thick mud.

Invisible, breathable, thick mud?

But his right arm. Still free—for the moment.

Justt facing the wrong way—for the moment.

Or not.

Another bestial growl. Behind his head. Hot breath sliming down his neck. Again.

"Juliet! Surrender and submit to me, Captain Killjaw! Or the boy dies here and now!"

Juliet flinched. Clearly struggling to stay standing. Resisting the heavy weight of those shackles. Even as they hung lower and lower.

Inches from the floor.

"W-W-What?!" Juliet said. "I-I-I. Sorry Roo. I. I. I."

Uh huh. Juliet helped Roo more than enough.

Well. Tried.

Time to repay her. But timing.

Critical.

"Fight to stay free," Roo said. "Fight to the end, and beyond!"

Juliet flinched, looking up toward him. Gorgeous serpent eyes staring shocked.

"W-Wha," Juliet said,. "Really? You 🤍 I ... I will 🤍 🤍 🤍 "

And Juliet clearly tensed with strain and effort. No holding back.

Despite shackles weighing her down even more.

Until the next bestial snarl. Still behind Roo.

"Then your girlfriends ..." Captain Killjaw said, "let' just say mermaid sushi sounds very good right about now ... cut fresh and screaming!"

Juliet gasped.

Yelped.

Crashed down to her bare knees. Head low. Shackles down, on the floor before her knees.

"NOOOOO ❣" Juliet said. "No❣ No❣ No❣ Don't hurt Bubbles❣ *Please!* I-I-I💔 I ... I ... I'm sorry Roo💔 Really sorry💔 I know you tried but I💔 I💔 I, Juliet Heartequin, sur—"

His left hand. Roo covered her mouth.

Quickly.

Shocking her to sudden silent. Enough to prevent her from swearing any magically binding oath and going familiar for that wretched Killjaw.

"Trust me," Roo said. "Don't move. At all."

And wide-eyed, Juliet nodded.

So that instant Roo slashed down at Juliet—at her right cuff. All his power behind the blow.

Slicing through it like a chief knife through watery mud.

Clank!

Blade hitting the floor.

"Hey!" Tinsel said, "Watch where you swing me, you jerk! That hurts!"

Tinsel ... was the blade? Crooster. He must have made a deal with her. Made her into a spellblade.

No time.

Killjaw. Huffed. The air around Roo. Scolding hot.

To his sides ... orange and amber flames?!

Killjaw. Those hot breaths. They were fire.

Not just air.

Fire.

His uniform—so many direct hits. It would only last so much longer.

His chest. Something. Powerful. wrapped around. Squeezing his. his chest.

Powerful.

His breath.

Gone.

Already gone.

His body. No. Coiled around it. A powerful snake-like creature, or limb. A foot thick and all brawn.

Squeezing tighter. And tighter.

And tighter.

"Squirm, boy," Captain Killjaw said. "Squirm! Squirm! Squirm!"

His vision.

Darker.

And darker.

"The time witch is **mine**," Captain Killjaw said. "All MINE!!!"

CHAPTER 19
RŒ DE BLADES

Time. witch? Juliet? What the … No.

Walled. In. Both sides walls. Of orange and amber. flame. Roiling walls. of flame. getting hotter. and hotter.

Cackling. louder. and louder.

Closing. in more. and more. around. Roo. Toward Juliet.

Juliet still. Knees on ground. Left hand shackled.

Right before him.

Her only hope—Roo. Roo shielding her. Shielding her.

Until.

Until.

Not. much. longer.

No.

No. time. left.

Until. Roo. with all. his might. another powerful. swipe. down at Juliet. at that other. black iron cuff.

Sliced off.

"Juliet ..." Roo said, "you're ... free! Now. magic. and **escape!**"

"No 💟 I won't 💟 " Juliet said. "We're friends, right? I'll save you 💟 "

Killjaw howled. Enraged beyond belief.

"NOOO!!!" Killjaw said. "You're mine! After all that work. Rumors of witches! Vanishing monsters. All for this moment! To trap the best familiar—"

With a fierce grimace Juliet shouted. "Familiar this, you creep 💟 💟 💟 "

Just as she shoved her palms up against the coiled creature.

"Return to thee egg," Juliet said, "from whence you came, Killjaw 💟 💟 💟 "

Next instant. The creature. Gone?

Just like the walls of flame.

Gone.

In Juliet's hands was suddenly a round egg the size of a melon. Colored dingy orange and spotted with amber and ... wait. That egg. A kind of dragon kind. Just like what ... maybe attacked him.

Killjaw ... was now an egg?

Then ... time witch meant ... Juliet could control time in some fashion and wow, that might be a crazy powerful magic to wield.

Roo gasped. "Air ..."

Just as Juliet tossed that egg aside. It hit the ground but

didn't break. Dragon eggs weren't exactly fragile. It just rolled harmlessly away.

Hopefully far away.

"Creep 🤍" Juliet said. "Grow up better next time 🤍"

Just as Roo gasped again. "Air ..."

Juliet hopped up to her feet. No a hint of weakness in her now. Her recovery. Really really quick.

Good.

Roo gasped one more time. "Air ... is nice."

Just as Juliet pecked Roo on the lips.

"As nice as you are," Juliet said.

Her smile as wonderful as the rest of her now.

CHAPTER 20
ROO DE BLADES

Silence.

Just nice and wonderful silence as Roo and Juliet smiled happily at each other. Gazing into each others eyes. Hers so much lovelier than the beautiful cloudless sky above them.

The sun blazing down on them. The gentle breeze from the window opposite of the cell door.

Neither had anything on the silent warmth between Roo and Juliet now.

Even with the hint of awkward in it. A cute adorable hint.

Even inside this cozy block of a dungeon cell.

Alone.

Together.

And sure, the wall next to Juliet, to each of her sides, the once-white wall was now charred black from the walls of flame that had been smashing into it. Clearly that had been the fire breath of the now egged dragon, Captain Killkaw.

Even the smell.

Not just Juliet and her wonderful but mysterious strawberries and vanilla candy scent but the smell of roasted stone. Of charred clothing. Of singed hair.

His hair. Singed.

Very singed.

But so what?

He was alive and well—and free.

Just like Juliet now too. Not a hint of singed hair along her wedges of hot-pink hair. None. No hint of charred cloth anywhere on her lovely but stunningly skimpy outfit. Not even her beret, let alone her skirt.

Nothing.

Not even a single burn.

Her hollow heart buckles for her chest belt and ultrashort and ultrasnug skirt. They both glittered nice and brightly. Almost blindingly brightly.

A nice bright though.

His dad. His mom. They'd definitely be proud of how this mess turned out.

Especially how Roo helped Juliet and her lovely blush of red spread from her dimpled cheeks down her slim neck and even across her shoulder and lower ... across those stunningly ginormous breasts of hers.

All no doubt from excitement mistaken for embarrassment.

All so very cute.

Almost too cute to handle.

Almost.

Especially when Juliet giggled so playfully happy. Wiggling in excitement too.

"So ..." Juliet said, "will you be taking me in, Missster Exorcist? I **so** surrender ... I **am** guilty of scheming to steal all of Twin Pearl's candy, he-he 💋 So search me all you want 💋 "

She even winked playfully at Roo. Hands held up before her ginormous chest.

So with a equally playful smile Roo slipped his free hand, his left hand over hers.

"Ooo I'll search you, you naughty little witch," Roo said. "And search even little sexy nook and cute—"

Crooster cawed from right above Roo. A caw that echoed freely around not just the cell, not just the hallway, but outside the dungeon, outside the window and ceiling.

Proving the strange echoes were gone and done with.

Then, with a flap, Crooster landed cozy on Roo's left shoulder.

Sigh.

So close to some sexy fun time and yet so far from sexy fun time ...

"Get a room, you two," Crooster said. "**After** we finish our business here. Don't forget Tinsel here needs time to adjust to being your spellblade too. She's already fainted, and won't wake up for a while."

But Juliet. She clearly wasn't deterred. Not at all.

"Aaaww 🤍 " Juliet said. "What a cute crow 🤍 🤍 🤍 "

"Ah," Crooster said, "one lady here has fine taste. Just like those friends of yours."

"You mean," Juliet said, "you found Bubbles and Felicia?! Are they safe? Are they—"

"They're headed this way," Crooster said, "last I checked. That Killjaw threw caution to the wind when he came here, and rescuing lovely ladies from peril is part of our duty too ..."

"Even ..." Juliet said, "us monster ... girls?"

Roo gave her hands a gentle squeeze.

"Saving innocent monsters," Roo said, "is just as important as stopping violent ones—it just ... doesn't pay nearly as well—"

Juliet pecked Roo on the lips again.

"Who says," Juliet said, "the reward ... can't be even better?"

Her hands now fingering the belt over her ginormous chest.

So Roo kissed Juliet back. "Best reward ever."

His fingers joining hers in their next adventure.

About the Author

Widely traveled, Jonathan Evan Hudson spends as much time studying life as he does writing gripping tales of fantastic adventures. From the giant redwoods of California to the deserts of Israel, his thrilling stories all draw on first-hand experiences and expand them with the fantastic and his acclaimed creativity.

Be the first to know!
For the updates and more:
www.JonathanEvanHudson.com

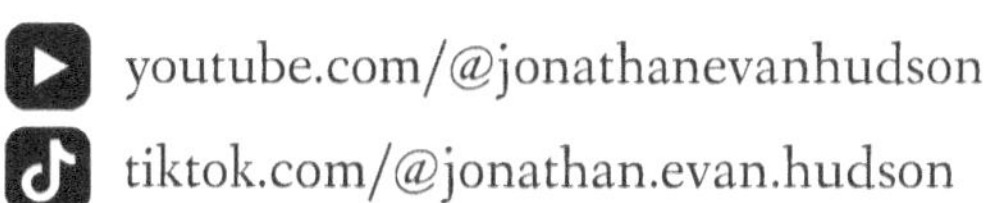

youtube.com/@jonathanevanhudson

tiktok.com/@jonathan.evan.hudson

A War Of Lust And Oak

Read Now!

✝ The Elf Girl Effect

Read Now!

The acclaimed Jonathan Evan Hudson once again weaves an unforgettable tale brimming with spicy page-turning action and fast-burning enemies-to-lovers passion.

Meet the newly knighted Roo Vorshaya. Sworn to protect humanity in the isolated mountain town of Appleharth. Dreams of action-packed adventure and passionate love under a lovely but sinister strawberry-pink sky.

Love re-ignited by a whiff of the familiar peaches and cream scent of his long-lost childhood girlfriend: the notorious elven witch Amber Peaches.

And endangering everything Roo holds dear.

Love page-turner novels of epic fantasy? Love reading from dusk to dawn? Then go read *The Elf Girl Effect* now!

Martial Art Of The Phantom Saber

Read Now!

Succubus Slash

Read Now!

The acclaimed Jonathan Evan Hudson weaves an unforgettable tale of thrilling action and adventure spiced with fast-burning romance and doused deep in epic fantasy.

Enter Miles Mayhem. Rich in friends and enemies. And a fat boy badass in the sword.

A seriously delicious smell of bacon and eggs smothered in spiced razor-hot cheddar signals celebration—and serious trouble ahead.

Trouble beyond anything Miles ever expected.

The perfect epic fantasy novel. A genre-enlarging feast for fans of sexy action and fabulous adventure. Read *Succubus Slash* now!

Sword Master Of Honey Heart Resort

Read Now!

Into Shadow Forest

Read Now!

A diamond in the rough the bestselling Jonathan Evan Hudson weaves a thrilling tale from explosive beginning to satisfying end in the awe-inspiring land of Grandcrest.

The talented twenty-something sword master Romeo Bladell yearns for love and adventure.

And at the musty edges of Shadow Forest. Near the towering high oaks bearded like stout old dwarves. By a canyon like a wound gnashed deep through in the granite. A canyon like the maw of a stone dragon.

A strange unexpected rope bridge hangs silently. Sinisterly.

Beckoning adventure—and danger unimaginable.

Enter *Into Shadow Forest* and savor the most spectacular of page-turning epic fantasy novels. Love unique monsters, riveting battles, and fantastic femme fatales? Then read *Into Shadow Forest* now!

Angels Of The Sword

Read Now!

Crossing Of Shadowed Death

Read Now!

The acclaimed master of fantasy Jonathan Evan Hudson once again shines through with his talented story-telling. Time to enter another stunning awe-inspiring world of dangerous demons, magical mayhem, and action-packed adventure.

A simple demon-hunting mission. The young and lonely Dirk yearns for amazing adventure, for gorgeously under-dressed dancer girls among the towering high ferns. Among the even taller pines of the hot and humid Fern Shadow Forest.

Pine needles everywhere. And so fragrant they made the finest of teas.

Sturdy reliable cobble roads of the Divine Empire cut through the whole entire forest. Providing the only safe passage.

Or so Dirk thought …

Enjoy this sexy, action-packed epic fantasy adventure from the talented Jonathan Evan Hudson. Love to read an enthralling epic fantasy novel full of stunning rip-roaring battles with creative new monsters? Then go read *Crossing of Shadowed Death* now!

A TASTE OF THE ELF GIRL EFFECT

The acclaimed Jonathan Evan Hudson once again weaves an unforgettable tale brimming with spicy page-turning action and fast-burning enemies-to-lovers passion.

Meet the newly knighted Roo Vorshaya. Sworn to protect humanity in the isolated mountain town of Appleharth. Dreams of action-packed adventure and passionate love under a lovely but sinister strawberry-pink sky.

Love re-ignited by a whiff of the familiar peaches and cream scent of his long-lost childhood girlfriend: the notorious elven witch Amber Peaches.

And endangering everything Roo holds dear.

*Love page-turner novels of epic fantasy? Love reading from dusk to dawn? Then go read **The Elf Girl Effect** now!*

CHAPTER 1
ROO

The sky was a strawberry custard for the eyes, and the same color of the lips Roo yearned to kiss.

So what if the clouds behind him were dark and ominous? The wind gusty and chilled more than the perfect shot of vodka. The taste of rain electrified by lightning-to-be ...

The street was as slim as his chances of success.

The cobble as bumpy as the journey ahead.

And this hill — a steep ascent into danger.

Roo even wore a jerkin woven of the finest dragon scale the son of ~~an~~ thee Exiled Exorcist of Most Notable Notoriety could hope to earn as one of the last members of the Vorshaya Clan.

Yup.

The Vorshaya clan. The once very badassed clan nearly wiped out to protect the greatest of the great Oak of Ages, a source of lightful magic and all from ... something, something he'd hunt down and deal with.

Still, if his mother hadn't been doing scholarly stuff far away at the time ... if she hadn't taken him with her ...

Sigh.

He didn't like to think about it much.

But his jerkin was pale blue as the sky ... wasn't today.

But it was one only worn by the best of the best True TriCross Knights. The big, white triple cross on his chest proclaimed it for all to see.

And a chance to pursue his dream to travel the world.

Slay monsters and save people, without any of that bounty hunter nonsense either.

Explores things, places that no one's ever explored before, or okay, more like no one's explored in living memory ...

Or longer.

His jerkin, it even had the snazziest, puffiest shoulder guards of the palest, bluest cold silver, and they were so so perfectly round that a certain Motherly Scholar of Notable Nagging couldn't hope to find a single fault with.

Just like the trusty pouch she made for him.

Shaped like a chubby triple cross, it was strapped to his waist and she magicked it to hold far more than you'd think it could and weigh so much less.

And just like his pouch, his slacks were as blue as the sky ... wasn't ... today.

And ... okay okay.

Anyways, his boots, and girls were obsessed with footwear or else the boot merchants wouldn't cater to girls so utterly much, so anyways, his boots were a snazzy dark blue suede, like the coming night sky should be (but obviously won't be. Pink sky meant severe storm coming.)

And with the coming storm ...

There were even spooky tentacles of mist rising from the street, and that only happened when a serious storm was coming through.

But the not so distant rumbles ... wasn't only thunder.

So not much time left ...

Good thing he wore a pair of sabers and a whip. One saber was of the bluest, sharpest cold silver, and the other, the blackest, sharpest cold steel, a stronger variant of cold iron, and the whip was made of pretty strong scarlet dragon scales, with the dragon magic woven strongly within the whip.

Good for offense and defense, against magical and nonmagical trouble too.

Sort of.

As long as he didn't whip his eye out, like his mother often teased.

Even more important, his trusty arm guards were both cold silver and cold steel forged together. His left arm guard could extend into a shield. The right held a miniature bow with a string of holy blue magic so that, with the right motion flicking motion, it would fire bolts of holy blue light or unholy violet light.

Perfect for a True TriCross Knight.

His heart raced for the coming battle.

For the girl she would soon save.

Since nothing, absolutely *nothing* raced a heart like that

elven fragrance, that whiff of the sweetest of peaches and cream only moments ago in this sweet sweltering hot afternoon.

No doubt about it.

The elf girl of his wildest dream come true. Right now. Here in the sexy flesh ...

Amber Peaches: a lust dream come true.

No.

Thee one and **best** lust dream come true.

And the muddy road here was a nice reminder of years ago, back when Peaches and Row got to quipping each other and their quipping got so fierce it broke out into mud wrestling that if, today their reunion broke into mud wrestling, wow, that would be so sexy amazing ...

Sniiiiiiiff.

It smelled ... surprisingly fresh. Earthy forest mud, no, soil fresh.

The lampposts at the street corners ... they were cold iron. The blackest of cold iron and forged like incredibly narrow, but tall, tulips of utter moonless midnight black.

Ah.

The oil lamps on top were those genie-style lamps to be wicked for the evening and wow, did they make the olive oil merchants rich.

But ... it was the genies inside that kept the mud clean. Kept their lamps lit at night, but what those genies were ...

Elf girls captured and lamped into genies due to the war between humans and demons, and well, elves were demons after all, and elves were the fully evolved form of fairies.

Even Peaches.

But the rumble of distant thunder that wasn't thunder was almost louder than his own tummy rumbling for some peaches and cream pie, especially after that sexy whiff of long missed Peaches.

(All better to tease Peaches with too.)

((Sure, elves should thank the Light their natural body odor, after lots of sweaty work, was so fruity nice rather than so gut-wrenching stinky like humans, you know, like him, but either way, frequenting the public baths, a necessity, human or elf.))

(But not first date material.)

((Outside of certain smut rags kept hidden under the best lock and key in an undisclosed location.))

(((*Very* undisclosed.)))

Even now, the sun was still as blonde as Peaches' waist-long hair, so no worries.

Last they ran into each other, back before war and puberty tore them apart, her hair was ass-long but also far far messier.

Just like back then, she styled the bangs to fountain off the sides of her head like gorgeously floppy wings, plus a floppy witch hat of rosy pink, that, of course, would hide her huuuuge but adorably pointy elf ears.

Ears so long and pointy, that resembled a cross between kitty and fawn ears, especially how they always were moving about so expressively.

So all in all, he wasn't so distracted by her fine ass in a finer minidress, (and it was the ultra-short, ultra snug and stretchy kind that was like strawberry custard to the eyes, ears, and loins,) so no, in that critical moment, he didn't walk into a wall.

No.

He walked into a door.

And as the Light would have it, there was plenty of wall he could of walked into.

The stone floors of the half-timber houses all along this block. All painted as colorfully as a field of wildflowers, but full of apples, apple blossoms, and even more apples.

This town was called Appleharth for a reason.

A very good reason.

And the door he did walk into was the usual solid sturdy oak, so no worries, it took the beating well.

Sure, there was ... a crack down the middle of the door now.

Sure. From him.

But the door's paint job was still spectacular.

No clumsy clod could hope to ruin those artful swathes of banana streaks full of cherry swirls. In fact, there wasn't even a nick to show for his clumsy moment.

Other than a wide crack down the middle.

And by the hinges too.

Roo credited his snazzy cowl and mouth cloth for softening the blow. They were as pale blue as the sky ... wasn't ... today.

But they were the color of Peaches' bright blue eyes ... well, last time they ran into each other years and years ago, over a decade ago. More than a decade ago. Wait. Same thing. Okay.

Good.

Dazed but not confused. A door would not stop him.

Or delay him.

Much.

Now one more chance or else ... he'd regret it for the rest of his life.

CHAPTER 2
PEACHES

Totally fucking ... that poster of parchment ... those blocky black letters spelling WANTED ...

Oh, for the Oak of Ages ... Peaches totally fucking wanted to give the middle finger to that sly sneak of a trickster the moment she spotted that parchment poster hanging all cozy and sinister and sooo much like a little black widow on those shutters behind the windowsill of those stinkier than stinky roses.

The sky wouldn't be the only one growling soon.

Good thing Peaches wore her finger loop gloves snug and ready. Each was as scarlet red as she'd soon make that trickster, what's her face, the Rouge Reapist, and even better, there were pentacles of unicorn hair woven into each palm to speed up her magic casting faster than a fox pouncing a mouse.

Along the glove were cute heart-shaped gaps. Normally, they'd hold rosy pink hearts, each of which held a precast spell she could fling at a target for instant effect, but she ran out a while ago and seeing a human alchemist ... pretty dangerous when her kind made such good ingredients to those sorts.

But that thunder close by, not just thunder.

The narrow street echoed the rumble and only confirmed the groan of a dire ogre coming this way.

Strange how there weren't any screams.

Disturbing, in fact.

Regular people shouldn't be so calm around one, unless ... no.

Peaches didn't want to think of it.

Yet.

It was bad enough that the pink sky, as lovely as it was, meant the coming storm would be terrible, if her father's stories held any truth to them.

(Big if.)

But no telling what these half-timber houses were hiding then. So what if they were beautifully decorated with apples, apples, and more apples? Plus a flower or two.

A chill seemed to ache her whole spine.

A warning of danger.

Demonic danger.

Nearby.

Never mind elves were technically lightspawn, a kind of demon, but of the light, so too many humans, sigh.

Least she usually could be reborn a few more times.

More than a few, actually.

Nine lives, like a cat, but three already used, but least her power and beauty were upped each time, but she started out as a brand new fairy, hatching from the Oak of Ages, and had to find another compatible human girl to fuse with, eat her soul and sigh.

No wonder some human despised demons of   all sorts.

If her brother only had one life ... if she only had one life ... like these humans ... sigh.

Why Roo even understood way back when ... sigh.

But the lamppost of black iron, horribly styled like tall and narrow tulips, no, that burn to their smell, a burn like that death pepper chili that little brat Roo tricked her stupid bratty self into trying long ago (and stupid her tried it again and again and again ...)

But it was definitely cold iron.

A quick way to a really, really awful death.

No wonder she couldn't pinpoint the source of demonic danger.

No doubt it was darkspawn demons but so what?

This was just a step toward her true dream, becoming an elf witch explorer, and discover why there's so many ruins appearing here and there, and elves had extension records proving some of these ruins appeared without a civilization before, as if it had been moved there.

Some even came from the future.

Others were from the distant past. Ruins that should no longer exist.

Ruins full of monsters.

So today, good practice.

Peaches made a point to keep strutting down the road without hesitation or obvious concern.

If orcs were hunting her ... letting them know she sensed something suspicious, especially as a witch with her foresense able to detect danger and ill intent toward her, well, according to her training, a big no no.

And despite it being in the early afternoon, the shutters of all the half-timber houses were shut.

Locked.

Other human towns she'd been in ... plenty of dumb human girls overlooked her demonic side and drooled over her looks, but here, today? Nope. Not one dumbass to brush off.

Something was off.

Good thing she could summon her bow and arrows of light quicker than any other elf in her generation, guy or girl. Several split seconds ahead of the best of the best guys and rapid fire better too. She could even build up plenty of blessed arrows as long as she got enough sunlight during the day, each day to build up and store more blessings for arrows for when she'd need them.

At least if any orc managed to get too close, the stiletto heels of her thigh boots could double as slyly placed daggers.

Alicorn style. Beauty and power came together for elf girls, so lucky her.

And her alicorn was the high grade spiraled kind.

Her boots were as scarlet red as she'd made those orcs.

Normally, she had rosy pink hearts lacing them snug up her leg. They normally would hold spells she could fling off for instant magical attacks just like her gloves.

But right now, like her gloves, they were just a bunch of heart-shaped gaps.

At least her rosy pink minidress and witch hat were woven with silk of a spellbinder silkworm. They weren't protective against blade and fang, or even against magic ... but they both together were a huge reserve of extra magic that naturally refilled as long as she wore them enough, especially in sunlight.

Even today.

And to fuck with the mind of those perverted orc bastards, she went with the sluttiest minidress she could manage. Translucent silk, so the right angles, the right nude elf deluxe, he-he.

So double the weirdness that no human guys went lusty dumbass toward her today.

Not even the gate guards.

Okay. Gate guards rarely did. Being a guard was all repu-tation and honor, not about coin. Any act tarnishing that, tarnished all the guards, and the guard loathed that.

Plus, her rosy pink minidress had the perfect distract and destroy notch down the front. One that showed far more than the little it covered.

Including her bra of ruby hearts.

And her chest, buxom to the extreme.

With only a few stretched to the breaking ruby ties down each the notches, the slutty side notches revealed more than just her tasty midriff, they revealed a good solid hint of her lace panties.

Ruby lace.

Orcs were rapeholic monsters, after all. She might as well use their lust smitten idiocy against them.

Roo would so laugh and approve.

(And leer.)

((Leer plenty.))

(((Sigh. *Boys*.)))

((((But if he didn't ... her pointy tipped boots, his rear, he-he.))))

WANT MORE?

Go to

WANT MORE?

Go to

www.JonathanEvanHudson.com